2 Picture Books by
Carol Fenner

2 Picture Books by Carol Fenner

Tigers in the Cellar and Gorilla Gorilla

Written by Carol Fenner

Illustrated by Carol Fenner and Symeon Shimin

AN AUTHORS GUILD BACKINPRINT.COM EDITION

AN AUTHORS GUILD BACKINPRINT.COM EDITION

Published by iUniverse, Inc.

For information address:
iUniverse, Inc.
5220 S. 16th St., Suite 200
Lincoln, NE 68512
www.iuniverse.com

Originally published by Harcourt Brace

Ensure copyright info for BOTH books is included: Tigers in the Cellar: © 1963 by Carol Fenner;
orig. published Harcourt Brace; LCC 63-7895. Gorilla, Gorilla: © 1973 by Carol Fenner;
illustrations © 1973 by Symeon Shimin; orig published by Random House; ISBN 0-394-82069-X

ISBN: 0-595-17555-4

Printed in the United States of America

TIGERS IN THE CELLAR

TIGERS IN
THE CELLAR

Story and pictures by Carol Fenner

For Phyllis
who can make magic
and Karen
who can hang by one leg

Once there was a little girl
who believed there were tigers
in the cellar.

In the daytime,
while she was busy
being a lady trapeze artist . . .

or an invisible secret agent
or teaching her baby brother to walk,
she didn't believe it
so much.

But at night,
when it was dark
and she was lying in bed,
she was sure she could hear them,
prowling and growling
in the damp, dark cellar,
growling and prowling and sniffing
way down underneath the house.

She would sit up and hold her breath
and strain her ears,
listening in the night.
When she couldn't hear them any more,
she would lie down.
But before long she could hear them again.
So she would sit up
and do the whole thing all over.
She sat up, she lay down; she sat up,
she lay down.
It took her a long time to go to sleep.

When she told her mother there were tigers in the cellar,
her mother said, "Nonsense,
there are only peach preserves and currant jelly
and potatoes in the cellar. And apple butter and
old empty jars. And there are cobwebs and probably
some comfortable spiders. But there are no tigers in the cellar.
Tigers are across the ocean.
In Asia, I think," said her mother.
Then she added sensibly, "Now go pick up the clothes
in your room."

So the little girl felt better all day.

But that night she heard them again,
growling and prowling
in the damp, dark cellar.

She sat up and held her breath.
She strained her ears and listened.
They had come from across the ocean.
When she lay down, she could still hear them,
prowling and growling and sniffing—
way down underneath the house.

It was a long, long time before she went to sleep.

The next day when it was sunny
and she was an invisible secret agent
and her mother was in the kitchen,
she decided to look in the cellar.

She opened the cellar door.
It smelled damp and dark.
She turned on the cellar light,
and it only smelled damp.
She went down the splintery old stairs.

There were peach preserves and currant jelly along the wall.
There were potatoes in the bin. She saw apple-butter jars
and empty jars. They were covered with cobwebs.
She saw one lone spider spinning a lonely web.

She checked very carefully for tiger prints.
But there were no tigers.

So the little girl felt better all day.
When she went to bed, she fell asleep right away.

But in the middle of the night
she woke up.

Everyone was asleep. Her mother and father
were asleep. Her baby brother was asleep.
Her dog was asleep in the kitchen
behind the stove. It was very quiet.
Probably the spider in the cellar was sleeping, too.

And then she heard them...the tigers...
growling and prowling and pacing
with their soft padded feet on the damp stone floor
of the cellar.

She sat up and listened, and then she couldn't hear them.
She tiptoed to the door of her room and listened.
She couldn't hear them. She opened the door and crept out
to the head of the stairs. She crouched in the dark...
listening and listening.

And then she heard them again,
prowling and sniffing. She heard
the cellar door being nosed open and padded feet
slipping through the house. She could smell
tiger smell, and when she looked down the stairs...

THERE THEY WERE.

At the foot of the stairs were two tigers.
Their yellow eyes were looking up at her.
They were very quiet. She was very quiet.
Then quietly, one of the tigers started up the stairs.

She didn't move. She didn't speak.
She tried very hard to be invisible.
The tiger moved like water over stones, and his feet
made hardly any sound.
His yellow eyes were on her face.
There was tiger smell
everywhere.

And when he was so near
she could touch him if she put out her hand,
he stopped.

She could see his moist nose breathing.
She could see his whiskers breathing.
She could feel his whole self breathing and
waiting. And waiting.

And then she saw,
rolling from his yellow eye,
a big tear.

She looked.
Another tear rolled from the other eye
and wiggled down the fur on his face.
She stopped trying to be invisible.
Slowly she put out her hand
and touched his furry face.

"Poor tiger," she said.
Tears came out of her eyes, too,
and wet the blue roses on her nightgown.
"Poor sad tiger."

The tiger put his head down and sniffed her toes.
He licked her toes.
He rubbed his head against her feet.
He rubbed his furry head against her feet until
the other tiger downstairs began to sing,
"Rumbly tumbly, rumbly tumbly," in a funny tiger voice.

Very high and very loud he sang:
    "Rumbly tumbly,
    pull my toes.
    Rumbly tumbly,
    rub my nose.
    Cobwebs on
    the currant jelly.
    Scratch my ears
    and tickle my belly.
    Stripes of yellow.
    Stripes of black.
    Climb upon
    a tiger back."

And the little girl climbed onto the sad tiger's back.
They went down the stairs and out the front door.
They rode all over the lawn, and then
they rode into town and up and down the empty streets.

The singing tiger loped beside them, singing,
"Rumbly tumbly." The street lights shone,
and the little girl's nightgown blew about her legs.

> *"Stripes of yellow.*
> *Stripes of black.*
> *Cross the ocean*
> *in a sack."*

Up the night streets they rode
where no one was,
and out of the town they bounded.

Trees hung dark and watching above their heads.
They flew across fields that were pale
and tiger-striped in the moonlight.
The wind rushed past them, and meadow grass
tickled the little girl's legs.

Up hills and down hills. Better than a trapeze.
"*Rumbly tumbly,*
the moon is pale.
The wind is quick
on a tiger tail.

"Cross the ocean
in a sack.
Ride on the night
and then go back,"

sang the tiger.

"Rumbly tumbly, and then go back," sang the little girl.
And back they went.

She was very tired when she got into bed again.
As she was falling asleep, she could hear the tigers
padding back to the cellar through the house.
"Cobwebs on the currant jelly," she heard.
"Scratch my ears and tickle my belly."
The cellar door closed,
and she fell asleep.

"I rode on one of the tigers last night,"
  she told her mother in the morning.
"There are two. One of them is terribly sad,
  and the other one sings."

"What a funny dream!" Her mother smiled.
"It wasn't a dream. They had yellow eyes, and I could *smell* them,"
  said the little girl.
"Nonsense," said her mother. "You dreamed it in your head
  while you were sleeping. Now go pick up your clothes."

The little girl went to the cellar door and opened it.
It smelled damp and dark and nice down there.
There was no tiger smell.
"Tigers!" she called down into the damp, dark cellar. "Tigers!"
There wasn't any answer.
"Rumbly tumbly," she whispered down the stairs.
There wasn't a sound from the cellar.

She knew that if she went down the splintery old stairs,
she would find currant jelly
and peach preserves and potatoes in a bin
and cobwebs and a spinning spider
and some old empty jars.
She knew she wouldn't find the tigers there.

"But it wasn't a dream at all," she told her mother.
"I hope the tigers don't think it was. I hope
they come back."
"*Please* go and pick up your clothes," said her mother.

Very slowly the little girl started up to her room.
She didn't feel like being a trapeze artist
or an invisible secret agent.
She took off her shoes on the stairs
and tried walking
like water over stones,
but it just made her sad.
It was going to be a disgusting day.
And she had to pick up her disgusting old clothes.

"Stripes of yellow.
Stripes of black."

She sat down on the stairs
and hummed to herself:

"Rumbly tumbly,
the moon is pale.
The wind is quick
on a tiger tail."

"It was not a dream
because I remember the song,"
she thought. And she sat on the stairs,
remembering the song.

"Rumbly tumbly,
way down below.
How many songs
does a tiger know?"

She gave her head a shake.
Those weren't the words.
Those were different words.
And while she sat there,
others came tumbling into her head.

"Uncurl your fingers.
Loosen your toes.
Unlock the songs
a tiger knows."

"Tigers?" she asked,
looking about her.
They couldn't be far away.

"Scratch my belly.
Tickle my ear.
A barrel of apples
and a tiger tear."

And then she thought the sad tiger
must be crying again
because the song stopped.
"Don't cry, tiger," she whispered.
She closed her eyes
to make it like nighttime.
"Don't cry." She thought it very loud
in her head
so the tigers would hear her,
no matter where they were.
"I'm always here," she said.
"Rumbly tumbly, I'm always here."

And she always was.

Gorilla Gorilla

Gorilla Gorilla

by Carol Fenner

illustrations by Symeon Shimin

For Faith

with whom I still share
a wild and gaudy
special sister laughter

He was born, wet and tiny
and gray,
one wet and gray morning
when the mists lay heavy in the rain forest.
His mother carried him close
in her big arms,
warm in her glossy hair.
His mouth was open a lot.
His appetite was endless.

Before many months
he could ride on his mother's back,
clutching
the hairs on her shoulders
while she moved about with the others,
feeding among the wild celery and thistles
or in the places of bamboo.

He grew.
His hair became long,
covering his body.
He learned which leafy greens
were tasty
and where to find the tender parts of bamboo
and wild celery.

Every evening he watched his mother
pull young tree shoots
and leafy bushes toward her,
bend and trample them
with her powerful feet
to make their nest for the night.

She arranged smaller leaves
and bushes about her,
and when she settled down
her great weight pressed the springy branches
into a mattress beneath her.

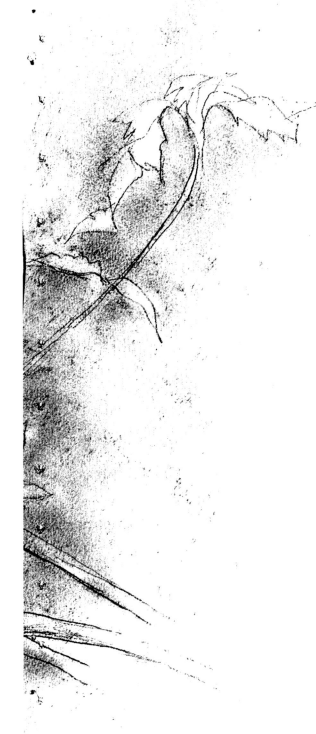

Soon he could make his own nest—
sometimes in a tree,
bending the leafy branches under him—
sometimes on the ground.
But he always left his little nest
to crawl in
beside his big warm mother
and sleep nestled under her arm
or against her round, rumbling belly.

He grew.
Sometimes during the day
he rode on his mother
while the group roamed
through the wet, dense forest
or fragrant meadows,
feeding.

But other times
he walked by himself on the ground,
pulling up his own food,
staying near his mother.
He looked for the prickly thistle
and ate it—
flowers, leaves, prickles
and all. He looked for
nettles and blackberries
and their leaves,
sweet herbs, bedstraw,
and the tender insides of wild celery.
He tried everything.
What he didn't like he spat out.

He grew.
He watched the bigger young ones
wrestle.
When he was a year old
he began to play with them,
to wrestle and roll and
follow the leader.

He was no longer the smallest
in the group.
Now there were new ones,
littler ones,
watching him.
He liked to climb and swing from vines,
to somersault,
to slap his chest
and kick his legs,
to walk across his mother's belly.

Day followed day.
Mist in the morning.
Sometimes rain
sliding off his back as he huddled
with the others.
Sometimes sun
warming their dozing bodies,
gleaming in their blue-black hair.

They kept moving always.
They followed the wild celery
and berry bush, followed
the silvery back of their huge leader
with his great arms
and stiff, crested crown.

The young one grew and grew.
By the time he was three
he was sleeping in his own nest
most of the time.
There were moments
during the browsing
drowsy days
when he felt a tickling excitement.
Then he would toss up leaves and branches
into the air
with quick and furious energy
like the older males.
He began to watch the silver-backed leader
more closely.

One afternoon
when the drops of a brief rain
were still on the leaves,
he noticed a sound,
a soft repeated hoot.
He had heard it before
but it had always been an unimportant noise
like vague and distant thunder.
Now he listened with a new curiosity.
The hoots grew louder and more rapid,
filling him with excitement.

He stopped chewing. He dropped a leafy stalk
he had pulled up
and followed the sound. The swift hoot-hoot
seemed strange to him
in his fascination
yet, at the same time, it was familiar
like the other sounds of the forest.
It came from the clearing where the group rested.
The females and youngsters had pulled into a cluster
at one end. The grown males
paced at the edge near the trees.

In the center of the clearing
sat the great silver-backed one,
his head thrown back,
his lips shaped around the beat
of the sound.
The young one did not join the others
but climbed for a better view
into an overhanging tree.
The air trembled with the silverback's swift hooting.
The great leader reached out
with a light swing
and plucked a leaf from a nearby bush.
He placed it like a flower
between his long, flat lips
and continued to hoot.

The hoots grew louder and faster,
faster and faster still.
Suddenly the huge leader
thrust himself to his short legs.
He tore up great clumps of bush and vine,
tossed them with a furious heave
high into the air,
and began to thump his massive chest
like a frenzied drummer.
The drumming boomed and leapt
into the leafy jungle,
across the high meadows
and jutting cliffs of the rain forest—
an increasing chorus of beats.
The hoots melted
into a blurred growl.

In the meadow
a black buffalo raised his head,
listening.
Birds flew up protesting.
As far as a mile away
a little red forest duiker
bounded nervously into the brush;
a leopard paused in his stalking,
nostrils to the wind.

The young one watched,
the half-chewed food forgotten in his mouth.

Suddenly
the great silverback dropped to all fours
and ran furiously sideways
thrashing his arms and ripping at the ground.
A youngster
who had strayed into the leader's path
was knocked off its feet.
A wild swing of his great arms,
a violent thump on the ground,
and it was over.
Quiet.
The sun shone undisturbed
through the heavy trees.

The bowled-over infant stood up,
shook its head,
and looked around for its mother.
The young one
sat in the tree for a long time afterward,
slowly chewing,
his excitement melting
into the drowsy afternoon.

He was to witness the great silverback's display
with increasing fascination
many times after that.
When the group had been disturbed
by the odor of men
or other groups like themselves
or some excitement he was too young
to recognize,
he came to expect
the leader's violent and compelling ritual.
He began to imitate the lordly crouch,
the great roar.
He even tried the whole kingly ritual himself,
learning to thump the hollow song
from his own expanding chest.
Sometimes
after the mists
had risen and left the forest,
he felt great happiness
in his body.
Then he, too, would thump his chest and toss
great clumps of leaves
high and joyfully into the air.

Day followed misty day
with rains and occasional sunshine.
His hair grew long, blue-black,
and glossy.
He could swing his long arms
and lift himself at a run
into the trees.

He often slept in the trees now,
his nest roughly woven of bent-in branches,
that rested in the crotch of the tree.
His brow had grown jutting
and fierce,
but his eyes were still soft
and brown
like his mother's,
like all their eyes.

When he was eight years old
he was almost full grown.
He was big for his age
and very handsome.
The young females
slapped at him playfully.
Young males avoided him.
On his crown
grew the beginnings
of a stiff, tufted crest
like that of the silver-backed leader.
His body had taken on the heavy muscles
of the young male.
The great silverback began to notice him
with cautious interest,
sensing in the younger
the stirrings of a future lord.

He weighed close to 300 pounds.
He was strong and glossy
and magnificent.

When the hunters came
into the eastern Congo
they were looking for magnificent animals.
They wanted healthy specimens,
young ones.
They wanted the best.
They came from another continent
across the seas.
They wore many clothes
and carried loud weapons.
They hired local trackers,
men from the villages,
to help them catch the wild animals
of Africa
for the people of another continent
to look at, and marvel.

They caught the leopard
and the lion in the bush of the lowlands.
They took the giraffe
from the high grass range,
the hippopotamus from the river bed
and the elephant who had come there to drink at dusk.
And they came into the rain forests
of the highlands,
looking for the mountain gorilla.

It had been an uneasy day,
a close, heavy day
that waited for rain.
The great silverback had led his group
deep among the trees for the night.
They built their nests
with slow, heavy movements
and dropped to sleep.
The young one felt lonely
and disturbed that evening.
He built his nest on the ground
to be closer to the others.

He was awakened abruptly,
jolted from deep in his sleep
by the blood-tingling scream
of the great silverback.
At the same time
he felt the faint slap
of something dense,
yet light,
fall down about him.
Rain?
A web of frozen air?
A net!

The hunters trapped the young one
with a net
among the trees of his own misty forest.
The warning screams of the others
as they escaped
came too late.
With terrifying strangeness
the net closed around him.
He tried to rise but the net tightened,
toppling him from his feet.
He tore at it; he ripped.
He couldn't find his balance.
The more he tore and thrashed,
the more his balance seemed to fail him.
He pulled his own hair in his frenzy.
He heard the great silverback roar and
beat his chest.
But finally
the huge leader dove into the trees,
followed by men making noise
with sticks and guns.

He felt himself lifted,
swaying dizzily. His stomach heaved—
his weight no longer belonged to him.
He struggled blindly in the net.
Then his body touched the floor of a truck.
He was in a cage. Bits of his broken nest
still clung to his hair.
He pounded his big chest
in fury and fear; he grasped
the bars of the cage
and shook them in his powerful hands.
The enemy net was still caught across his shoulders.
"He's a beauty," said one hunter to the other.
And they drove him away
while he raged with the tangled net
in the back of their truck.
From somewhere
deep in the forest
the silverback screamed his warning
over and over.

After a day of sickening travel in the truck,
he was loaded aboard a transport jet
and taken across the ocean
to another continent.
The motion of the plane
made him listless and ill.
He lay on his back
with his legs sprawled
and his soft eyes fixed on the ceiling.
He did not move
except to roll his eyes
toward the man who brought his food.
He did not eat.

All around him was the close smell
of other animals.
Sometimes the tight, helpless growl
of the panther in the next cage
made his sprawled legs twitch.
But he did not move from his back.
When the jet landed,
the big ape's cage
was lowered from the hold
into another truck.
The unfamiliar smells and sounds
of this strange place
made him roll up to his feet.
He clutched the bars of his cage
and peered from under his fierce brow
at the new shapes of things,
at the pale, choppy faces of people.
He was bewildered and his body ached.

They took him
to a large zoo.
He was put into an indoor cage
with an outdoor yard
surrounded by high walls and a moat.
There was a tall tree in the yard.
The moat was full of water.
They put a sign
in front of his walled yard.
It said, "Gorilla gorilla beringei,"
and underneath it said,
"Habitat: East Africa."

Gorilla gorilla
did not go outside
into his walled yard.
He lay on his back
in his cage
on the cement floor
with his legs sprawled,
his soft eyes fixed on the ceiling.
He did not eat.

Next to his cage
was a shaggy red orang-utan
who liked apples.
On the other side
were three baboons
who quarreled among themselves
and showed off
for the people
who looked into their cage.

Gorilla gorilla lay on his back
in the indoor cage.
He did not eat.
He stared at the ceiling.

One day
the long, shaggy arm
of the orang-utan
reached through the bars
for Gorilla gorilla's uneaten apples.
Gorilla gorilla turned his fierce brow
toward the orang-utan.
His eyes were angry.
Immediately he rolled to his feet
and slapped the shaggy red arm away.
Orang-utan leapt back with a scream.
Then Gorilla gorilla ate.
He devoured his food.
Later he sat in a corner of his cage
glaring at Orang-utan.

After that he always ate his food.
And sometimes
he went outside into his walled yard
to lie on his back
by the single tree
with his legs sprawled,
staring at the sky.
His hair
began to grow glossy again.

In the afternoons
when school children came to the zoo,
he would lift himself partway
through his door
and leave only his back end
for them to see.
This was not very interesting
to the children.
They always moved on
to the baboons,
who made them laugh with their tricks.
Or they watched Orang-utan,
who climbed about
showing off his shaggy red hair.
No one found Gorilla gorilla
magnificent.

On Sunday afternoons
the zoo was always full of people
peering into the yards and cages.
The panther paced,
restless and frustrated.

The baboons did their tricks
so they could watch the people laugh and clap.
Orang-utan
displayed his amazing shaggy grace.
Sunday was a lively day.
The people watched the animals.
The animals watched the people.
There was clapping and laughing
and the chattering of many voices.

Only Gorilla gorilla
refused to see the people.
He leaned halfway through his door.
All anyone could see of him
was his broad backside.

One day
Orang-utan next door
was moved to another cage.
It took the keepers
all morning to get him out of his old cage.
They finally tempted him out with apples.
For several days
the cage next to Gorilla gorilla
was empty.
He had just begun to miss
his shaggy red neighbor
when the keepers brought in
someone new.

The new one
was another gorilla,
a young female.

Gorilla gorilla watched them
bring her in.
She was sick and listless.
Once inside her cage
she lay on her back
with her eyes on the ceiling.

Gorilla gorilla lay on his back, too,
but occasionally
he stole glances at her
from under his great brow.
Eventually
he stood and paced his cell a while.
He stopped near where she lay in her cage.
He sat down.
She did not move
or look at him,
but he liked the smell from her cage.
It was a familiar smell.
It awakened dim feelings in him.

Fresh rain,
new wet leaves, and damp old wood,
dead trees fragrant with rot and rain . . .
and he smelled his mother
and sun on dozing bodies.
He sat there
with the feel of the rain forest
moving in him.
Old ways stirred his blood . . .
the spongy spring of soft ground
beneath his feet, mossy trees,
and the stretch of his arms
as he lifted himself swinging.

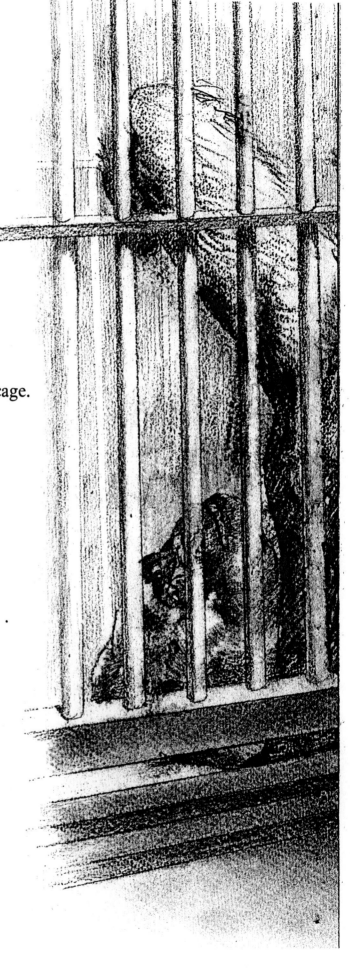

He sat there
immobilized with pleasure,
the warm presence of the long ago group
about him.
In tantalizing snatches
dimly he seemed to hear
the old safe sound
of the great silver-backed leader
snoring in the night.
Inside his chest
an aching swelled.
He rolled restlessly to his feet
and lumbered outside.

It was nighttime in his yard.
He squatted in the darkness,
his soft eyes staring at nothing.
He smelled the great cats
in their close cages.
He heard them twitch
and cough.
He smelled birds on the wind
and elephants swaying on their legs.
The hippopotamus snorted,
and he heard it.
Inside the cage next to his
the young female gorilla
lay on her back,
staring at the ceiling.
Gorilla gorilla's chest ached—
it seemed to him
he was close to home.

The next day was Sunday.
People came from everywhere
to look into the yards and cages.
Parents lifted their children
up high to see.
They threw peanuts
to the elephants.
They watched the panther pace
and the lion lie like a lord.
The baboons made them laugh and clap.
It was a lively day.
The people watched the animals.
The animals watched the people.
There was clapping and laughing
and the chattering of many voices.

As usual
Gorilla gorilla stood half in
and half out
of his doorway.
The young female gorilla lay on her back
inside her cage.
She had eaten nothing.
She did not seem to hear the noise
of people outside.
To Gorilla gorilla
the noise was bright and irritating.
The ache in his chest
swelled.

He looked at the young female.
Her hair
was dull and shedding
and her body
a brooding heap.
She did not admire him.
She was not even curious.
She lay on her back staring
at the ceiling.
Gorilla gorilla stood
halfway through his doorway,
ignored
at both ends.

The noise of people continued
to bother him,
a bright clutter of voices, a scuffling
of feet.
The sounds confused themselves
inside him,
mixed up together
with old sounds he had known.
Sunday sounds of the zoo,
or was it the jungle stirring?
The shrill shout of a child,
or was it a sunbird against the dripping trees?
He heard the caged cat yawn,
the tread of the black buffalo,
the elephant crashing through the brush,
the ice cream vendor, the scolding nurse,
the golden monkey flying through the rain-wet trees,
the rustle that was wild animals
listening
and the jungle growing.

Gorilla gorilla's chest was bursting
with old stirrings
and a new, bewildering ache.
He lifted himself from his doorway
and with a startling heave of his huge bulk,
he turned.
There were gasps from the crowd of people
who had been watching the baboons.
Gorilla gorilla stood leaning
on his knuckles,
staring at them
from under his fierce brow.

The crowd rustled and whispered,
watching the great ape.
Children
pointed their fingers.

Gorilla gorilla sat down slowly;
slowly he tilted his head back.
He parted his lips
and began a low hoot-hoot-hooting,
his gaze fixed in the distance,
like a great silverback
sitting among the vines and bushes
of the forest.
Carefully and deliberately
Gorilla gorilla reached out and plucked a leaf
from beneath his single tree
and placed it delicately between his lips.
The crowd watched,
hushed and waiting.

Then with a startling movement
he hurled himself up and into the tree.
He began to climb,
ripping and tossing branches
as he went.
The crowd gasped
and backed away.
Gorilla gorilla lifted himself
with powerful, easy swings
to the very top fork of his tree.
He stood.
His big hands lifted
and fell,
drumming
against his vast chest.
Again and again.
The deep beat boomed
flat and hollow through the air.

In their cages
the big cats heard
and paused in their pacing.
The elephants heard.
Hippopotamus raised his heavy head.
Inside her cage
the female gorilla
rolled to her feet.
She lifted her head,
her nostrils suddenly alive.

The crowd was silent,
watching the big ape
in amazement.
His huge hands
beat out an ancient sound
against his bursting chest.
Behind him
the sky was pale.
He stood, lifted to his full height
against the light.
"What a magnificent animal!"
said a woman in the crowd.

He stopped drumming
and swung violently to the ground.
He ran furiously sideways,
his huge arms
thrashing out.
He stopped
abruptly
and thumped the ground.
Some people in the crowd
jumped.
It was over.
Quiet.
The sun shone undisturbed
in the pale sky.
They watched him amble to his tree
and sit.
He leaned against the trunk.
He seemed to doze.

Inside her cage
the female gorilla paced.
She was hungry for the first time
since her capture.
She ambled around and around
restless for food,
restless for Gorilla gorilla to return
from his yard
so that she might greet him—
might look into familiar softness
of brown gorilla eyes.

The afternoon grew old.
Children became hungry.
Mothers' and fathers' feet hurt.
Like a sigh
the people began to drift away,
remembering their homes.

Gorilla gorilla
dreamed
against the tree,
a pleasant dream
in which he moved feeding
with the others
among the wild celery and thistles
and in the places of bamboo.

Author's Note

I would like to extend a special thanks to two gentlemen:

George B. Schaller, whose *Year of the Gorilla*
(University of Chicago Press) provided me not only with
facts in my research, but sights, sounds and smells of
the mountain gorilla in his forest.

Jiles B. Williams, my husband, whose excitement over
a magnificent gorilla in the Ueno Park Zoo in Tokyo prompted
the book to begin with.

Carol Fenner Williams

Carol Fenner 1998
Photo by Jay Williams

CAROL FENNER was born in 1929 in the town of Almond, a small village in upstate New York She began making stories as a four-year-old, before she could write. Her delighted mother would take down the words.

Her first two published books were picture books which she also illustrated. *Tigers in the Cellar* (1963) and *Christmas Tree on the* (1966) were centered in and around the century-old house of her early years. Surrounded by wide lawns, a vegetable garden and orchard in back, the search for a Christmas tree began and ended at the back door with the journey in between through the orchard, across railroad tracks, climbing lower slopes and upward until, after trials in the cold winter day, a Christmas tree was discovered.

The tiger song in *Tigers in the Cellar* was based on a memory of her father who pulled little Carol and her younger sister, Faith, across the bumpy lawn in a wagon shouting, "Rumbly tumbly! Tangerino! Beanerino!"

"It was such a lovely, lively, silly song that it stayed with both my sister and me." says Ms. Fenner.

A root cellar under the old house, where her mother kept apples, potatoes, onions and home canned fruits and vegetables, was also a home for spiders and their cloying webs. And there were noises. Snakes slithering? Mice scampering? Something breathing? It became the setting for *Tigers in the Cellar.*

"I don't think the cellar exists anymore," said the author. "The house is there but it is unrecognizable now. There's a deck and a swimming pool. The maple tree my father planted when my brother, David, was born has been cut down. But maybe the cellar is still there; maybe the tigers still creep up those splintery old steps to the cellar door and listen. Maybe a small child will one day let them out to romp through the night."

The afflatus for Ms. Fenner's fourth book, *Gorilla Gorilla,* "attacked" her in Japan, first on a holiday where she and her husband, Jiles B. Williams (Jay), an air force officer, saw a magnificent gorilla in the Ueno Park Zoo in Tokyo.

"We saw him first indoors. There were a number of spectators in front of the cage. The gorilla was large and sulking, glowering from one corner of his cage where he sat. Unlike most gorillas I had seen in zoos whose coats are dull and shedding, this big guy's fur was glossy and healthy-looking. His angry eyes were very intimidating. My husband was not intimidated; Jay elected to glower back at the big gorilla. The next thing we knew there was a growling and the air electrified as the gorilla threw himself savagely against the bars of the cage and began to shake them. People screamed and involuntarily jumped back. Satisfied, gorilla pulled haughtily away from the bars and, in the humping kind of walk gorillas have, strolled back to the corner, sat and continued to glare at us all."

"'Did I do that?' Jay asked. And he did it again to find out - staring sternly at the gorilla. Instantly the beast leaped up with the awful sound and began to shake the bars again. Again the spectators shrieked and jumped away."

"'Could that *really* have been me?' asked Jay. And, naturally, he had to try it again."

"Jay and the gorilla enjoyed this game for a while until the rest of the folk watching began to glare at Jay, too. They may have thought he was being mean to the gorilla, but I think my husband was providing this caged animal with more diversion than he'd had in a long time."

The Williamses were so enamored with 'their' gorilla, that they went back to visit him. This time, he was outdoors and would only present his rear end to the crowd - his behind sticking out of his cave door, his head inside. "What splendid contempt he had for us," says the author.

Carol Fenner now lives in Michigan with her husband, Jay (Major Jiles Williams, USAF/Ret.) where her current books, all novels (*Randall's Wall*, *Yolonda's Genius* and *The King of Dragons*), take place.

AWARDS & HONORS
ALA Notable Book 1963 - *Tigers in the Cellar*

Runner up: **Coretta Scott King Freedom Award** 1979 (This wasa mistake as the awards committee assumed Carol Fenner was a African-American) Readers' choice master list - Nebraska - *The Skates of Uncle Richard*

1973 **Christopher Medal** for non-fiction; **Library of Congress Book of the Year** 1973; **Outstanding Science Trade Book for Children** 1973; **ALA Notable Book** 1973; proposed for Newbery Medal - *Gorilla Gorilla*

Readers' choice master lists in Arkansas, Connecticut, Indiana, Iowa, Kansas, Minnesota, Missouri, Nebraska, Oklahoma and Rhode Island. Winner: **Maryland Best Children's Book Award** 1997 - *Randall's Wall*

Newbery Honor Book 1996, **ALA Notable Book**, **New York Public Library's 100 Titles for Reading & Sharing**, Readers' choice master lists - Massachusetts, Missouri, New Mexico, - 1998-99- *Yolonda's Genius*

Paterson Prize (The Poetry Center) 1999-2000 **Notable Children's Trade Book in the Field of Social Studies** 1999 **Notable Children's Book in The Language Arts** 1999 Readers' choice master list: Vermont - *The King of Dragons*

GRANT: Michigan Council for the Arts Literature grant, 1982 to assist in the completion of a collection of short stories.

MEMBER: The Authors Guild, Inc., Michigan Council for the Arts Literature Panel 1976-79, Society of Children's Book Writers and Illustrators

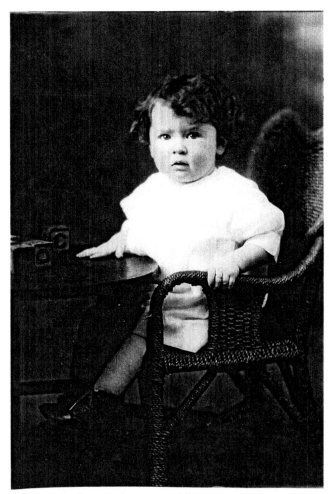

Carol Fenner - 1-1/2 years

Carol Fenner
East 17th Street, Brooklyn, NY
14 years old

Jay & Carol (Fenner) Williams
Dancing at the Bayview Gardens
Sept. 1998
photo by David King

Carol Fenner on Sassy Mac
Fall 1999 - Photo by Dee Lyne

Symeon (Semyon) Shimin

Credit Photo: Mottke Weissman
Late 1970's

Whether he was executing a painting or illuminating a book or designing a poster, "he was an artist from the time he was born," says Rosa Shimin, widow of the late Symeon Shimin. Shimin used the same imagination, grace and intensity on the beautiful books he drew for children that he spent on his paintings. He did not rush his work. When more than a year passed for his gorilla art, *Gorilla Gorilla*'s editor at Random House, Jenny Fanelli, says he would tell her, "They'll be worth waiting for." It took nearly two years. They were worth waiting for.

He was born Semyon Shimin in Astrakhan on the Caspian Sea, Russia, in 1902. When he was ten years old, his father, a cabinet maker and later a dealer in antiques, brought the family to this country to escape the Tzar. His daughter, Toby, repeats her father's memory that, on approaching Ellis Island on the voyage from Russia, he described looking out the boat's bow and seeing "a sea of hats".

His family established a delicatessen in New York City and Symeon worked there as a child. He began to draw on the brown paper bags used to wrap meat in. Later, at fifteen, Symeon went to work as an apprentice to a commercial artist and, after three years, he became a free-lance painter. Although he later studied art at New York City's Cooper Union and at George Luk's studio, he considered himself primarily self-taught. His major schooling was absorbed from the museums and galleries he frequented in New York City.

Toby Shimin says, "He was passionately moved by social issues and stories of struggle. His great hope was to paint a large mural on the theme of Liberation. He was a very proud man who possessed an almost magical charisma which touched nearly everyone he came in contact with."

In 1936, in a national competition, Symeon Shimin won an award and commission to paint a wall mural at the Department of Justice in Washington, D.C. He received citations from the U.S. Treasury Department for his 1943 War Poster and, in 1955 - 1957, the Certificate of Excellence from the American Institute of Graphic Arts. Another national competition awarded him second purchase award in the First Provincetown Arts Festival with the painting going into the permanent collection of the Walter Chrysler Art Museum in Provincetown, Massachusetts

Shimin became admired as a painter of independent thinking and perception. "He couldn't finish a painting before it was sold," remembers Rosa Shimin. In 1973, Lloyd Goodrich of the Whitney Museum of American Art wrote, "He is a highly gifted artist with a personal vision and style, who has never followed fashion in art but has consistently expressed himself in his own individual way."

Bennett Schiff, art critic for the *New York Post*, wrote of Shimin's painting, *Discussion Group*, "...beautifully organized, dramatic and most moving painting; notable for its controlled design, its power and its emotional impact. His draftsmanship is impeccable and his technical knowledge most delightful and admirable."

Symeon Shimin lived and painted in Rome in 1957 and Paris in 1975. His work as been exhibited at the Corcoran Gallery in Washington, D.C., the Whitney Museum of Art in New York City, the Art Institute of Chicago, the Brooklyn Museum in New York, the National Gallery in Ottawa, Canada and the National Gallery in Washington, D. C. Permanent collections include Walter Chrysler Art Museum in Provincetown, Massachusetts; Forbes Watson, Critic & Editor - *Magazine of Art;* Mme. Maria Martins, Brazilian Embassy; Fairleigh Dickenson University, Rutherford, New Jersey and various private collections.

Symeon Shimin is probably better know to the world at large for his illustrations in more than fifty children's books, including *How Big is Big?* (his first), *Zeely, Onion John, Sam, One Small Blue Bead, Dance in the Desert, The Island of the Blue Dolphins, The Wonderful Story of How You Were Born, Joseph and Koza,* and *Gorilla Gorilla.*

The many authors whose work he has graced include Byrd Baylor, Margaret Wise Brown, Carol Fenner, Jean Craighead George, Virginia Hamilton, Joseph Krumgold, Madeleine L'Engle, Scott O'Dell, and Muriel Rukeyser.

Mr. Shimin maintained a studio in New York City and spent his summers at Amagansett, Long Island, New York. He died in June of 1984.

Bibliography

Horizon - June 1941 - London

The Studio - July 1943 - London

American Painting Today - 1939
>   Published by American Federation of Arts, Washington, D.C.

Magazine of Art
>   Feb. 1939
>   Feb. 1940
>   Jan. 1942 New York

Architectural Forum
>   Dec. 1940 New York

Art News
>   Mar. 1940 New York

U. S. A. Vol. 2, Number 9
>   Published by U.S. Office of War Information

New York Times - Dec. 21, 1941

Coronet - Sept. 1950 - New York

Time Aug. 18, 1958

-57 **Awards**
>   Mural commission, Dept. of Justice, Washington, D.C. (Nat'l Competition, 1938)

Citations
>   U.S. Treasury Dept. 1943 - War Poster

Symeon and Rosa Shimin in his NYC studio 1959

Symeon at work in his NYC studio under the Brooklyn Bridge

Toby Shimin (Symeon & Rosa's daughter) with her daughter,
Sophia, September, 2000

0-595-17555-4

Printed in the United States
69610LV00006B/23

9 780595 175550